STECK-VAUGHN ◆ BOLDPRINT® kids

The Lion and the Mouse

An Aesop's Fable
Retold by Janine D'Ippolito
Art by Robbie Short

Literacy Consultants
David Booth • Larry Swartz

 www.rubiconpublishing.com

Steck-Vaughn is a trademark of HMH Supplemental Publishers Inc. registered in the United States of America and/or other jurisdictions. All inquiries should be mailed to HMH Supplemental Publishers Inc., P.O. Box 27010, Austin, TX 78755.

Common Core State Standards © Copyright 2010. National Governors Association Center for Best Practices and Council of Chief State School Officers. All rights reserved. This product is not sponsored or endorsed by the Common Core State Standards Initiative of the National Governors Association Center for Best Practices and the Council of Chief State School Officers.

If you have received these materials as examination copies free of charge, Houghton Mifflin Harcourt Publishing Company retains title to the materials and they may not be resold. Resale of examination copies is strictly prohibited.

Possession of this publication in print format does not entitle users to convert this publication, or any portion of it, into electronic format.

Copyright © 2012 Rubicon Publishing Inc. Published by Rubicon Publishing Inc. All rights reserved. No part of this publication may be reproduced or transmitted in any form or by any means, electronic or mechanical, including photocopying, recording, taping, or any information storage and retrieval system, without the prior written permission of the copyright holder unless such copying is expressly permitted by federal copyright law.

Editorial Director: Amy Land
Project Editor: Dawna McKinnon
Creative Director: Jennifer Drew
Art Director: Rebecca Buchanan

Printed in Singapore

ISBN: 978-1-77058-543-0
2 3 4 5 6 7 8 9 10 11   2016   22 21 20 19 18 17 16 15 14 13
A B C D E F G

Can **Mouse** free **Lion** from the **trap?**

CHARACTERS

With one quick turn, Lion grabbed Mouse in his paws.

Rooodaarrr!

Yummy! My afternoon snack!

"Why should I let you go?"

"If you let me go, I promise to help you if you ever need me."

Lion laughed and laughed.

"Need *you*? Ha! Ha! Ha! *You* will never be able to help *me*."

Well, Mouse, you are such a funny little fellow! I will let you go.
Off you go, Mini Mouse.

Help *me* indeed! Ha! Ha! Ha!
Just you wait! I'll *be* back, and you'll *see* that I *can* help you!

Later that day, two hunters set up a trap to catch Lion.

The next morning, while out looking for food, Lion noticed the trap.

What's this?

For teaching tips, see the BOLDPRINT® Kids Graphic Readers Program Guide at www.steckvaughnboldprint.com.

Comprehension Strategies:
Making Predictions
Identifying Main Idea/Theme

Common Core Reading Standards
Foundational Skills
3f. Recognize and read grade-appropriate irregularly spelled words.

Literature
1. Ask and answer such questions as *who, what, where, when, why,* and *how* to demonstrate understanding
2. Recount stories, including fables and folktales from diverse cultures, and determine their central message, lesson, or moral.
3. Describe how characters in a story respond to major events and challenges.
9. Compare and contrast two or more versions of the same story

Reading Foundations
Phonics: Consonant Digraphs, *ch, gh*
High-Frequency Words: catch, caught, free, friend, great, hard, head, kind, laugh, learn, morning, next, sleep, thank, way, woke
Reading Vocabulary: bet, brave, break, chewed, climb, dare, grabbed, hunters, lion, mouse, patience, promise, rescue, save, strong, trap
Fluency: Reading with Expression

BEFORE Reading

Prereading Strategy — **Activating Prior Knowledge**
- Read the title and take a picture walk. Say: *This story is a fable. A fable has talking animals and teaches a lesson. What do you already know about fables?*

Introduce the Comprehension Strategy
- Point to the **Making Predictions** and **Identifying Main Idea/Theme** visuals on the inside front cover. Say: *Today we'll make predictions about a story. Predictions are guesses based on clues in a book. We can guess to figure out the story's message, or main idea. Let's make a prediction about this story.*
- Point to the cover. Model making a prediction.
    Modeling Example Say: *As I look at the cover, I see some important details that might tell me the main message of the story. Lion is sleeping. Mouse is crawling over him. I see flies buzzing loudly, and Mouse is covering his mouth trying be quiet. This means Mouse doesn't want to wake Lion. He's probably scared of Lion. I predict Mouse will wake Lion, and Lion will eat Mouse! I predict the main message will be* Don't wake a sleeping lion!
- Draw a T-chart on the board labeled *My Predictions* and *Did It Match the Text?* Then write your predictions. Be sure to label your main idea prediction.
- Ask children to make and share predictions and write them in the chart.